Dragon
Time For a Picnic

Adapted by Ivy Silver
Based on an original TV episode written by Greg Dummett & Aline Gilmore

SCHOLASTIC INC.
New York   Toronto   London   Auckland
Sydney   Mexico City   New Delhi   Hong Kong

J

ISBN 978-0-545-20057-8

Dragon © 2011 Cité-Amérique – scopas medien AG – Image Plus.
Used under license by Scholastic. All rights reserved.

Published by Scholastic Inc. SCHOLASTIC and associated logos
are trademarks and/or registered trademarks of Scholastic Inc.

12 11 10 9 8 7 6 5 4 3 2 1   11 12 13 14/0

Printed in the U.S.A. 40
First printing, April 2011

68583

It was a warm and sunny day.
"It's the perfect day for a picnic,"
said Dragon.

Dragon met his friends at the park.

They were excited for a fun day.

"Let's play kick ball," said Alligator.
"I want to fly kites!" said Ostrich.

"Let's eat picnic food," said Dragon.
Beaver just wanted to take a nap.

"First let's play ball!" said Mailmouse.
"Who has the ball?"

"Uh-oh . . ." said Alligator.
"I forgot to bring the ball."

"It's nice and windy," Alligator said.
"Who has the kites?"

"Uh-oh . . ." said Ostrich.
"I forgot to bring the kites."

Beaver wanted to take
a nap in a hammock.

But he forgot to bring a hammock.

Dragon and his friends were sad.
They forgot the things they needed
to have a fun picnic.

Then Dragon had an idea.
"There are lots of fun things we can do
that don't need *things*!" he said.

First the friends played pattycake games!

*Pattycake, pattycake,
make me a treat.
Make me a treat
that's nice and sweet!*

Then they played a game of Beaver Says.
"Beaver says, Stand on one foot!"
said Beaver.

"Beaver says, Wiggle your head!"

"Beaver says,
Time for a nap."

And he fell right to sleep!

After Beaver woke up from his nap,
everyone was hungry.

"Uh-oh . . ." said Dragon.
"I forgot to bring the food!"

But Dragon had an idea.

They had a picnic lunch
at Dragon's house.

It had been a perfect picnic day after all!